THE MIGHTY EXPLORERS

JoGenii

# NANHA MOOSHAK SOLVES THE PROBLEM

RED PANDA

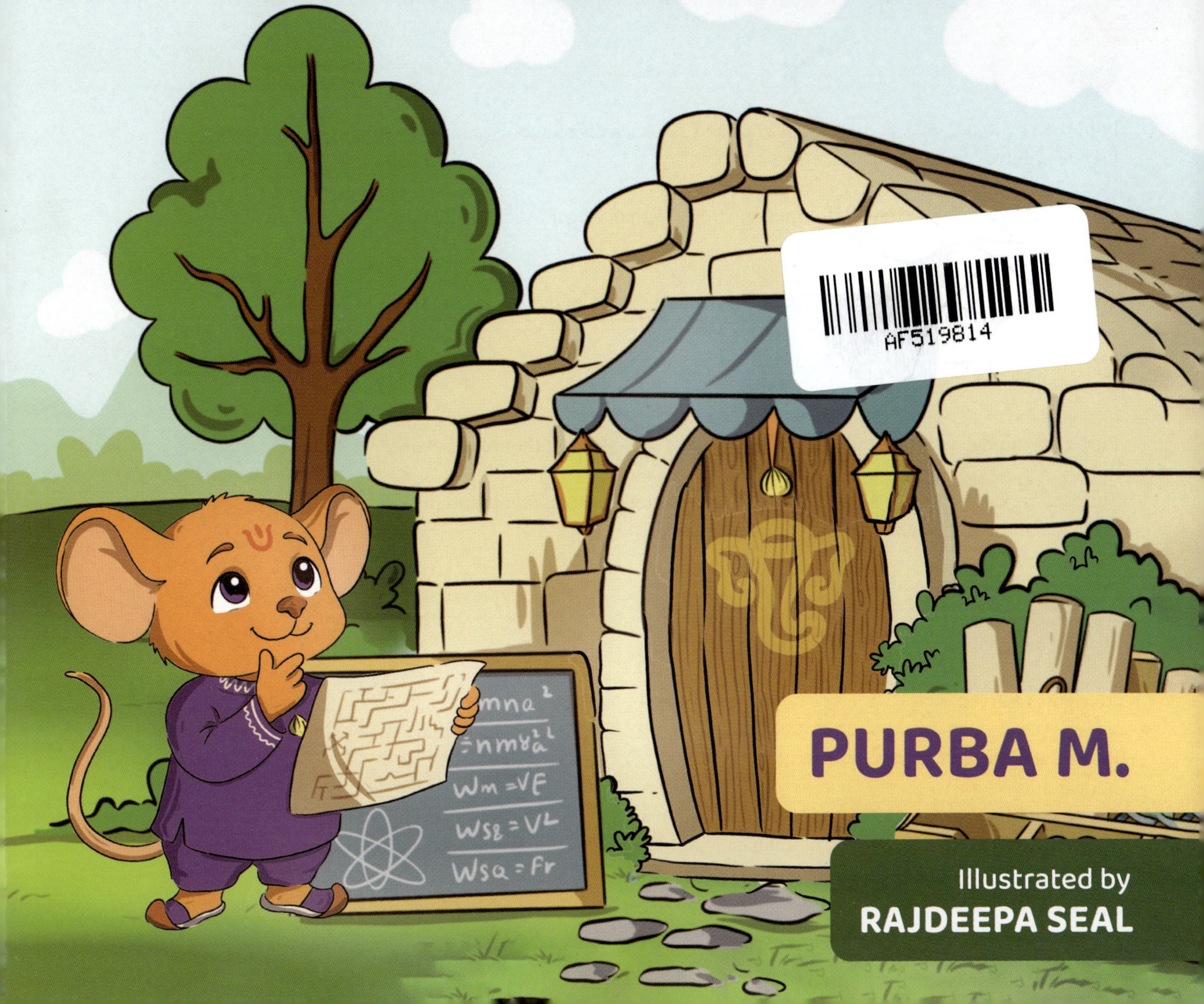



PURBA M.

Illustrated by
RAJDEEPA SEAL

*For Jojo and Koko, who make ordinary days shine.*

*For Sid, the calm behind my chaos.*

Published by Red Panda, an imprint of Westland Books, a division of Nasadiya Technologies Private Limited, in 2026

No. 269/2B, First Floor, 'Irai Arul', Vimalraj Street, Nethaji Nagar, Alapakkam Main Road, Maduravoyal, Chennai 600095



ISBN: 9789379859150

10 9 8 7 6 5 4 3 2 1



Printed at Nutech Print Services Pvt. Ltd.

Meet Nanha Mooshak,
Blessed by Lord Ganesha,
He is small in size but
big on ideas.

In Khojpur, where the gods' vahanas live and play,
Five super friends zoom around all day.
They are the Mighty Explorers of Khojpur—kind, brave and true.
Come join them, adventure awaits you.

Say hello to brave Bal Simha and wise Uluka Di,
Clever Nanha Mooshak and strong Veer Nandi,
Then there is the watchful Garuda Sen,
Together they all fly through sunshine and rain.

Now this is the story of Nanha Mooshak, you see,
The tiniest explorer, but as clever as can be.
While others rushed to push and try,
Nanha Mooshak gently asked, 'But why?'

He solved problems, clue by clue,
And found the path others could not view.

One sunny morning, happy and bright,
The Mighty Explorers planned a picnic with delight.
They packed their snacks and spread the mat,
But oops! The basket got stuck—just imagine that!

'I'll try looking from afar!'
Garuda Sen flew high.
'I'll try lifting it!' Veer Nandi tried.
They pushed and pulled and
tried once more,
But the basket stayed
stuck—just like before.

Bal Simha stepped up, brave and loud,
'I'll scare it out!' he roared aloud.
Uluka Di circled, then shook her head,
'That won't work yet,' she said.

Nanha Mooshak tapped his chin,
'Big strength isn't always how we win.'
He peeped at the rock, the basket, the ground,
And smiled at the clever little trick he'd found.

'Let's not lift,' said Nanha Mooshak with a grin,
'Let's roll it gently! Maybe that's how we'll win.'
He slid a smooth stick under one side,
Tip ... tilt ... roll! Yay, the basket began to glide!

The basket moved with a soft ka-plop!
Everyone gasped, then giggled and stopped.
'That stick' said Uluka Di, calm and clear,
'Is called a lever—it helped us here.'

'A lever helps when times feel tough.
It helps us move things big enough.'
Nanha Mooshak stood tiny, yet tall,
'Thinking smart can help us all!'

Uluka Di smiled and turned a page,
'Now hear a story from another age.'
'Long ago,' she read, 'on paths so wide,
Walked Lord Ganesha, calm and wise.'

‘One day a heavy stone blocked the way,
Too big to lift, too hard to sway.
Strong ones pushed with all their might,
But the stone didn’t move, left or right.’

Lord Ganesha's Mooshak, looked around,
Then smiled at something others hadn't found.
'We don't need to move it,' he said low,
'There's a clever way around, you know.'

Ahead, they found a narrow space,
A hidden path, a secret place.

Uluka Di closed her book with care.
'That's why Ganesha chose Mooshak there.
Not for his strength or size so grand
But for finding a smarter path at hand.'

Nanha Mooshak beamed, his whiskers twitched,
'Like me!' he squeaked, proud of all his tricks.

It's good to be like Nanha Mooshak, clever and small,
You don't need big strength to help at all.
When something feels tricky, pause and see,
Ask, 'Is there a smarter way for me?'

Big ideas don't need big size,
They shine when we think smart and wise.
A little thought can save the day,
That's the clever Nanha Mooshak way!

## ABOUT THE AUTHOR

**Purba M.** is a parent, storyteller and believer in compassionate parenting values.

Through her work with JoGenii, she creates story worlds and learning experiences that encourage kindness, courage and confidence in young children.

She believes that the bravest lessons are often the quietest ones—and that every child deserves stories that feel safe, warm and true.

## ABOUT THE ILLUSTRATOR

With a love for colours and curiosity, **Rajdeepa Seal** brings stories to life. She enjoys creating playful, imaginative visuals that invite readers to explore and dream.

Find more about JoGenii here:
www.jogenii.com

See more of the Mighty Explorers here:
https://www.youtube.com/@JoGenii